Scary Stories for Sleepovers

C.B. Colby, Ron Edwards, John Macklin,
Sharon McCoy, Arthur Myers, Margaret Rau,
Sheryl Scarborough

Sterling Publishing Co., Inc.
New York

Library of Congress Cataloging-in-Publication Data Available

10 9 8 7 6 5 4 3 2

Published by Sterling Publishing Co., Inc.
387 Park Avenue South, New York, NY 10016
© 2006 by Sterling Publishing Co., Inc.
Material in this book originally published in *World's Best True Ghost Stories*
by C.B. Colby, © 1990 by Sterling Publishing Co., Inc.; *World's Best Lost
Treasure Stories*, © 1991 by C.B. Colby; *World's Strangest True Ghost
Stories* by John Macklin, © 1991 by Sterling Publishing Co., Inc.; World's
Most Mystifying True Ghost Stories, © 1997 by Ron Edwards; *Scary Howl
Of Fame*, by Sheryl Scarborough and Sharon McCoy, © 1995 by RGA
Publishing Group, Inc.; *World's Most Bone-Chilling "True" Ghost Stories*,
© 1993 by Sterling Publishing Co., Inc.; *World's Most Terrifying "True"
Ghost Stories*, © 1995 by Arthur Myers, and *World's Scariest "True" Ghost
Stories*, © 1994 by Margaret Rau.
Distributed in Canada by Sterling Publishing
c/o Canadian Manda Group, 165 Dufferin Street
Toronto, Ontario, Canada M6K 3H6
Distributed in the United Kingdom by GMC Distribution Services
Castle Place, 166 High Street, Lewes, East Sussex, England BN7 1XU
Distributed in Australia by Capricorn Link (Australia) Pty. Ltd.
P.O. Box 704, Windsor, NSW 2756, Australia

Sterling ISBN-13: 978-1-4027-2182-3
        ISBN-10: 1-4027-2182-X

For information about custom editions, special sales, premium and
corporate purchases, please contact Sterling Special Sales
Department at 800-805-5489 or specialsales@sterlingpub.com.

Contents

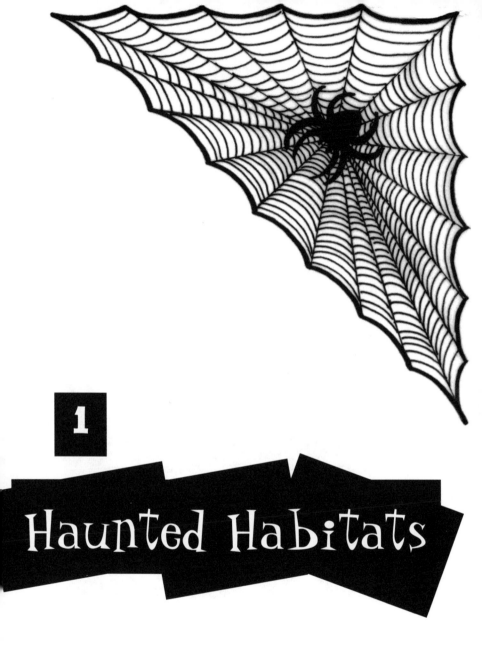

1

Haunted Habitats

Spook House

It had once been known as Spook House, the old building in Hydesville, Massachusetts. But the children playing there in November of 1904 had no thought of legends or ghosts, and it was a complete surprise when part of one wall suddenly collapsed. One of the children was practically buried. The others ran for help, and the owner of the house, William Hyde, and others went to the rescue.

They freed the child and then noticed that there was a hole between the fallen wall and the cellar foundation. In the hole they found a peddler's tin box and close to it the incomplete skeleton of a man. The head was missing.

This evidence settled once and for all a controversy that had raged in the previous century when a family named Fox lived there. They had claimed they experienced weird, ghostly happenings. Their story is one of the most fantastic occult tales of all time.

John Fox, a farmer, lived in the hamlet of Hydesville with his wife and two daughters, Margaretta, 13, and Catherine, 9.

They were a highly respected family, and until they moved into the house in 1848, their life was quiet and unexciting. Then it started. They began to hear inexplicable tapping noises, sometimes soft, sometimes very loud, as if heavy objects were being moved around. Both children became so frightened that their bed had to be moved into their parents' room. Then, the ghostly rappings became so loud and so violent that the beds shook as if an earthquake were rocking them.

The family searched the house, but could find no explanation. The ghostly tapping became progressively louder. Soon the family was completely worn out from lack of sleep.

One night when the noises began, nine-year-old Catherine clapped her hands and challenged the ghost to imitate her. At once her claps were repeated.

Then Mrs. Fox asked the spirit to tap out the ages of her children. To their amazement, the ghost immediately obliged. It even paused for a couple of seconds and then rapped out "three." A third child had died at the age of three.

Joining her daughter, Mrs. Fox asked the spirit to signal with two knocks if it was indeed a spirit, and there followed almost at once two distinct taps. Growing more confident, Mrs. Fox put more questions to the ghost, indicating the number of taps to be given for each specific answer.

In this way, she learned that the spirit was a man who had been murdered when he was 31, and that his body was buried in the cellar of the house. A neighbor, Mr. Duesler, put questions to the ghost, and learned that the killing had been carried out in a bedroom some five years earlier, with a butcher knife, and that not until the night following the murder was the body taken down into the cellar, to be buried ten feet under the floor of the house.

The spirit also rapped out the information that the killer had been motivated by robbery, stealing $500 from the victim. The cellar was dug up, but nothing was unearthed. This caused many people to accuse the Fox family of manufacturing the whole story.

The following summer, digging was restarted and this time evidence was found—traces of quicklime and charcoal, a plank, hairs, and pieces of bone that a doctor declared had come from a human skull. But no body was found.

Then came more unexpected evidence to support the Fox family's story. Lucretia Pulver, who had been employed as a servant by the former tenants, a Mr. and Mrs. Bell, said that one day a peddler, aged about thirty, had called at the house. She had seen him talking with Mrs. Bell, who claimed the man was an old acquaintance.

Lucretia was dismissed by Mrs. Bell that same day, but before she left, she asked the peddler to call at her home before leaving the district, because she wished to buy something from him. He agreed to stop by the next morning, but he never did.

A few days later, she was amazed to be offered her job back by Mrs. Bell. Returning to the house, she saw Mrs. Bell altering some coats, and several things from the peddler's pack were lying around the house.

Sent down to the cellar one evening, Lucretia fell on loose earth. She screamed and Mr. Bell proceeded to fill in what he told her were rat holes.

Lucretia also reported other strange happenings—ghostly rappings and other mysterious sounds. Soon after this, the Bells left the house.

Lucretia's story threw suspicion on Bell, but he was never charged, there being no definite evidence against him.

After the Fox family left, no one went to live in Spook House again.

Haunted Ferreby House

Sometimes greed reaches even beyond the grave. Perhaps this is what happened in the case of the mansion known as Hopsfield. It got its name because it stood in the middle of a field of hops outside the town of Waterlooville in Hampshire, England.

A huge, rambling Gothic-style house, it was built by a Ferreby in the early 1800s. Proud of his mansion, which boasted a long flight of stone steps to the front door, Mr. Ferreby was determined to have it stay in his family forever: It must never change hands. It would always be home to the Ferrebys. That was his dying wish.

The Ferreby offspring lived in the house and raised their children in it. But when the grandchildren were grown, and their parents had died, they wanted nothing to do with the old place. The rooms had always seemed dank and cold and the atmosphere was heavy and oppressive.

After moving out, the Ferrebys rented the house to a group of Spiritualists, who weren't there long before they began complaining that the ghost of old Mr. Ferreby kept appearing, shaking with anger and threatening them. They were so terrified that they asked for and received permission to sublet the house.

The new occupants were a widow and her daughter, then in her twenties. They stayed only a short while. The mother was found dead in her bed at one o'clock in the morning. Soon afterward, the daughter moved out of the grim old house, which by this time had begun to get a sorry reputation.

No one else wanted to rent the house. But the Ferreby heirs were able to sell it. It was bought almost immediately by a newly retired sea captain and his wife. One of the captain's treasures was a collection of Indian daggers he had gathered on his travels. He now kept them in a display case in the hall of the Ferreby house.

One morning the sea captain was found lying dead in the front hall, one of his Indian daggers buried in his back. His widow moved out immediately, leaving behind a mystery that the police couldn't solve. Only the local people claimed to know what had happened: Old Ferreby's ghost, long in his uneasy grave, was the killer.

By this time no local person would think of going near the old house. But in the 1920s it caught the eye of the Dalton family, who were determined to buy it even against the advice of advisors and friends. The old Gothic-style building appealed to Mr. Dalton. The dark gloominess of its interior, he said, was the result of neglect. The rooms could be renovated and the atmosphere improved. He poured money into the house, transforming it into a beautiful and luxurious home, but he was never able to get rid of the strange chill that seemed to pervade it.

Overnight guests of the Daltons remember uneasy nights—strange noises, doors that were opened by invisible hands, children who woke in the middle of the night to find themselves crammed under their beds. And everyone still complained of the cold, oppressive atmosphere that no amount of renovations could change.

But there was no discussing these things with the Daltons. They had ready explanations: Children do strange things in their sleep; old houses settle at night, making noises of all kinds; doors come open under the pressure of drafts. The dank, chill atmosphere was just the psychological effect of all those scary stories.

Then one summer Dalton's son, a brilliant young man attending Oxford—with everything apparently going for him—went into the basement of the old house with a gun and blew out his brains. A few weeks later his grieving mother died. Not long after that Mr. Dalton himself suddenly dropped dead in his dressing room. Only one child remained, a daughter. She moved out at once. The magnificently renovated house was boarded up and left empty. No one went near it now. Cold and grim, it stood alone in the field of hops. Did old Mr. Ferreby have his wish at last?

House for Sale

"**D**rive a little slower, dear," Therese Storrer said to her husband. "There's a house for sale."

Hans-Peter Storrer stepped on the brake, and the car slowed down, its spoked wheels brushing the roadside grass.

It was July 1908, and Therese and Hans-Peter Storrer were on the threshold of the strangest and most unaccountable experience of their lives. They were about to negotiate for a home of their own—with a family of ghosts.

The story of the Storrers, which unfolded in a village in the hills outside Vienna, has become a classic of Austrian psychic research. "Of all my investigations, this is the only case for which I can offer absolutely no rational explanation," wrote Dr. Paul Bonvin, a famous investigator of supernatural phenomena who died in 1925.

As the car coasted to a halt, Hans-Peter, a twenty-eight-year-old bank official, pushed up his dark glasses and examined the dusty "For Sale" notice.

The couple had been married for two years and had spent all that time living in the cramped flat of Therese's parents. They were searching anxiously for a house of their own, preferably in the country but reasonably near Vienna.

Hans-Peter swung the car around and started slowly up the narrow lane toward a house standing high above them on green sloping ground. As he drove, he noticed how grassed-over and lacking in recent wheel marks the lane was.

The observation meant little to him at the moment. Later it slipped starkly, logically into place. For dead men don't drive cars.

A few minutes later, they reached a set of open iron gates leading onto a weedy courtyard. The house, in pale flaking brick, stood across an overgrown lawn. It was neglected; its paint was peeling. But there was no doubt that it had once been an elegant house.

Hans-Peter stopped the car and helped his wife out. They

waited a few moments, but no one came to the door; no faces appeared at the window.

There was a curious oppressive silence, broken only by the couple's footsteps as they walked toward the front door.

Later, Therese recalled what happened next: "We stood at the door, and Hans-Peter knocked. We heard the knocks resounding through the house—an eerie sound—but no one answered. There were curtains at the windows, and there appeared to be furniture inside. We were quite sure the house was inhabited.

"Eventually, my husband tried the door. It was unlocked. There seemed little harm in having a quick look around now that we had gone this far. He went in first and I followed."

The house was dim and filled with cobwebs. The furnishings that filled every room were thick with dust, riddled with the ravages of moth and worm. In the kitchen, crockery and cutlery were laid out on a table for a meal that obviously had never been served. In the pantry, bread and vegetables, laid on the marble slabs, had long since rotted away.

All the trappings of living were there in the decaying, neglected house. Only the people were missing.

Therese continued the story: "By this time I was ready to leave—I wouldn't have lived there however reasonable the price. But Hans-Peter was determined to look over the rest of the place.

"We walked along a gloomy corridor and opened a door to what I assumed to be the main living room of the house. The door swung back and we both saw them clearly. There were people in the house.

"Heavy curtains hung at the windows, but there was still enough light for me to be certain of what I saw. There were four people in the room—a man, a woman, and two children. They were sitting motionless in chairs around the fireplace. It was like a weird tableau.

"After what seemed like hours—it could only have been seconds—they turned and looked at us. They were wearing clothes in vogue in the 1890s and the man held a silver-topped cane.

"Strangely, my first reaction was not one of fear or horror. I just thought how pale and sad they all looked ..."

Slowly, the image faded before the visitors' eyes and finally vanished completely. Not surprisingly, the Storrers wasted no time in putting as many miles as possible between themselves and the house on the hill!

It couldn't have been a hallucination, because they had both witnessed it. Afterward they separately recounted what they had seen, and the details tallied exactly.

It was over six months before Hans-Peter Storrer could bring himself to drive back to the village in the hills to seek an answer to the mystery that had been plaguing him. And he found it at the first place he visited—the tiny post office run by Ludwig Wahlen.

"That house, sir, has been for sale for nearly ten years," Herr Wahlen said. "There was a shooting tragedy up there. The master shot his wife and two children. It was in all the papers."

He rummaged in a drawer and produced a yellowed sheet of newsprint. A large photograph headed the page. Looking at it, Hans-Peter saw again the sad, pale faces of the dead family he had witnessed in the house on the hill.

The Haunted Cabin

Near an eastern entrance to Yellowstone Park in Wyoming, there used to be a crude log shack known as the Haunted Cabin. Here's how it came by that name.

The cabin had long been deserted, when one night, many years ago, a forest ranger camped in it. Just as he managed to fall asleep, he was awakened by a loud pawing and snorting nearby outside in the snow. It sounded as though some other ranger had ridden up on his horse and was about to enter the shack.

He lay there for several minutes while the noises continued. But no other ranger came to pound on the door. Finally he began to feel uneasy and, taking his gun, crept to the door and threw it open. There was no one there, neither man nor horse.

After lighting a lantern, he circled the cabin, but could find no tracks. Baffled, he went back to bed. Presently the snorting and pawing began again. Again he rose and searched the area around the cabin clearing, but to no avail.

The rest of his night was spent tossing and turning, trying to shut out the loud sounds from outside. The next morning he made still another search, found nothing, and left, glad to be away from the place.

15

Several other campers and hunters stayed at this cabin during the following months, and all sooner or later reported the same snorting and pawing sounds outside, although none of them had heard any rumors about a phantom horse and rider at the log shack.

Finally, after a restless night, one camper decided to investigate further. He researched the annals of the Yellowstone area in local libraries and discovered a newspaper account that may—or may not—explain the weird incident, but which was nonetheless intriguing.

The camper learned that many years before the first forest ranger reported the pawing sounds, a drunken cowboy had spent an extremely cold winter night in the cabin. He had tied his horse to the tree by the door and stumbled inside to sleep a frigid eight hours wrapped in his blankets. The horse, left uncovered and freezing outside, pawed and snorted to get free. The next morning the cowboy found his horse dead in the snow.

Perhaps the horse's ghost was still trying to get free from that tree. Or perhaps it was just coincidence that all those who stayed in the cabin seemed to hear the same sounds in the night. The incidents remain strange and baffling.

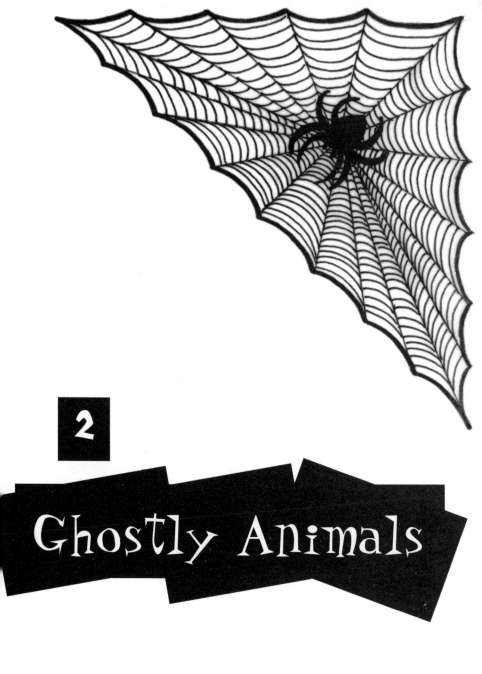

2

Ghostly Animals

Haunted by a Dove

Many years ago, in an Alabama village, there lived a man and his wife who were supremely happy together. After years of wedded bliss the wife became very ill and nothing could be done to save her.

On her deathbed she announced to the family and servants that she would return to the garden in the form of a white dove so that she could be with her husband in the place where they had known such true love and happiness. Moments later she died.

Years passed, but no dove appeared to carry out the dying wife's promise. Eventually the widower fell in love with another woman and decided to marry her and bring her to the big house to live.

On the day he carried his new bride over the threshold and into the house, a white dove came fluttering into the garden and perched upon a flowering snowball bush by the gate. It uttered long, low moans as though it were heartbroken.

Every afternoon the dove returned to moan and sigh on the snowball bush. The servants were frightened and upset. They thought that surely this meant that the first wife's promise was now being carried out!

Eventually the second wife heard the story, and she too became disturbed. Soon people from the village and from neighboring plantations came to stare over the garden wall at the dove on the snowball bush.

The new wife grew nervous and ill-tempered, and the happy home began to crumble. Legend or no legend, the husband wanted to preserve his new life. Frantic, he decided upon drastic action.

The next afternoon he seized his rifle and slipped from the house, stealthily working his way into the garden, where the dove sat moaning and sobbing. He raised his rifle and fired. A woman's scream answered the blast of the gun and the dove flew away, its breast reddened with blood.

That night, as the husband slept, he died. No one could determine the cause. His widow moved away to escape the tragic memories, and the great house fell into ruins.

The master of the house was buried by the snowball bush. His gravestone, they say, is still there, but there are no visitors—but one. For it is said that every spring when the blossoms of the snowball bush first open, a white dove with a red-splotched breast appears among them, moaning pitifully.

Night Ride

This story was told by an old doctor who lived a hermit's life in a small New England village. It happened when he was a young boy, but he told it and retold it in exactly the same way until his death.

When the doctor was fifteen years old, his father had a bay colt that he let his son ride. One evening the boy started riding to a nearby town. On the way he had to pass a cottage where a woman by the name of Dolly Spokesfield lived. She was rumored to have unusual powers, skill in the occult arts, and the ability to turn herself into almost anything she wished. She was, it was whispered, a genuine witch of the inner circle—certainly a person to be avoided by anyone out at night alone.

As the lad approached the cottage that belonged to Dolly Spokesfield he kept to the middle of the road and urged the colt to a faster trot. But his precautions were in vain.

As the colt and rider came abreast of the cottage, a coal-black cat suddenly leaped out of the darkness and landed on the colt's neck. The frightened horse stopped short, almost throwing the boy over his head.

The boy tried desperately to get rid of the cat and urged his mount on, beating him with his whip, but the cat held on and the colt refused to move with the vicious cat hissing upon his neck.

The boy was afraid to leave his horse and run. In panic, he dismounted and began to beat the cat with the whip, holding the colt by the bridle rein as it reared and plunged, trying to shake off the terrifying creature.

At last the boy dislodged the cat and hurriedly rode home. The poor colt was bruised and clawed, and apparently exhausted by his ordeal. So injured and frightened was he that the boy was afraid the animal would die before morning. He turned him loose in the barn instead of putting him in the stall, and went to bed trembling and fearful that the colt wouldn't last the night.

At dawn, the boy hurried to the barn to inspect the battered and clawed animal. To his amazement, the young horse was in perfect condition. He showed no sign of exhaustion, and nowhere on his body could the boy find a trace of bruises from the whip, a claw mark, or a single reminder of the frantic events of the previous night.

The story has an even stranger ending. A neighbor soon stopped by to report that Dolly Spokesfield had just been found almost dead, her body bruised and beaten as though by a whip. And under two of her fingernails were some short bay hairs, such as you'd find, perhaps, on the neck of a young colt ridden by a frightened boy alone in the night.

The Witch Cat of the Catskills

Spook Woods, a strange spot in the Catskill Mountains of New York State, deserved its name.

It was said that even dull-witted cattle who wandered into these woods would suddenly rush away in panic at what they had encountered. Certainly horses often balked at taking the road that ran through Spook Woods. The local people usually managed to go through it only in broad daylight, and preferably with company.

A farmhand named Williams, the story goes, had been hired to work on a farm on the other side of the woods from his home. Williams had heard tales of Spook Woods, as who up that way hadn't? But he was a big, rugged, and ordinarily fearless man who paid little attention to tales of witches and supernatural happenings.

However, one winter night as he returned home through the woods on foot, he did feel a certain uneasiness. It was only because of the full moon that cast odd shadows along the side of the dirt road, he reassured himself. But as he reached the center of the wooded stretch, he realized that one shadow was hurrying along ahead of him. This shadow was more than a trick of moonlight, for it was moving quickly over the snow along the roadside.

As he hurried to pass it, he saw to his astonishment that the shadow was made by two cats who were dragging another, obviously dead cat, between them. What a strange way for animals to act, he thought, as he quickened his steps. The cats hurried too and kept right up with him. Then, to his increasing horror, one of them called him by name.

Startled, he wouldn't—he couldn't—stop. The terrified man began to run, desperately anxious to get out of the woods as fast as possible.

The cats, slowed down by their burden, were unable to match his speed, but just as he was leaving the thick woods for the open country beyond, one of them screeched in a loud, clear, and almost human voice, "Mr. Williams, oh, Mr. Williams, when you get home tell Molly Myers that she can come home now. Old Man Hawkins is dead."

Terribly shaken by his experience, Williams raced home. Once he reached its warm, friendly atmosphere he hesitated to tell anyone about his harrowing experience. But later in the evening, when sitting with his family around the fireplace, he half-jokingly told about it, and finally repeated the odd message.

To everyone's astonishment, the old white cat lying by the hearth sprang to her feet, and without once looking back, leaped up the chimney right over the burning logs and was never seen again. Was that Molly Myers? Had she at last gone home?

3

Messages from Beyond

Drip, Drip, Drip

This eerie encounter is said to have taken place around West Chazy in New York State. Not long ago a local resident, deciding to go fishing in a nearby pond, dug himself some worms, cut himself a nice pole, and taking along his dog, clambered into an old flat-bottomed boat for a quiet afternoon.

The dog curled up in the bottom of the boat and fell asleep almost as soon as the man had baited his hook and tossed it over.

The fish weren't biting. The man rowed from one spot to another, trying first here and then there along the shore. It was

almost as though all of the fish in the pond had been caught or were in hiding.

Finally the man decided to try his luck in the middle of the little lake, where the water was deepest. The moment he anchored there, the dog, who had been sound asleep the whole time so far, woke with a start and began to whine and tremble.

The man spoke sharply to him, telling him to be quiet and lie down. The dog obeyed, but he kept whining softly and trembling violently.

Hardly had the man dropped his hook to the bottom when

he felt a tug. He began to pull on the line, but it seemed to hold fast to the bottom.

At this point, the dog jumped to his feet and began to bark viciously, showing his teeth and peering over the side of the boat, rocking it sharply. While struggling with the line, the man gave the dog a blow with one of the oars, sending him into the other end of the boat, where he cringed, whimpering.

Once more the man heaved his stout fishing pole. Slowly his catch—whatever it was—came to the surface. Tangled on the end of the line was a great clump of what looked like human hair. Shining in it was a bright golden barrette.

As the object appeared at the side of the boat, the dog let out a howl of terror and plunged into the lake, heading for shore. He soon made it to land and vanished into the woods.

The man was amazed at the actions of the dog, but nevertheless decided to take the hair home and give the barrette to his wife. She could use it, he thought, to hold her hair back.

The barrette was so entangled that they would need to hang the hair before the fire to dry out to make removal easier. His wife, though horrified at the idea, coveted the bright barrette and so consented.

Long after the strands of hair were dry, the sound of dripping could still be heard.

It went on all evening. Then, at the stroke of twelve, a woman's voice came from the hanging strands. It told of her murder and how her body could be recovered. Then the voice faded away and was heard no more.

The man and his wife couldn't believe what they'd heard and decided to keep it to themselves for the time being, particularly so that the wife could keep the valuable barrette.

However, the dripping sound continued. It went on all night and all the next day, and the day after that. Finally, they could stand it no longer and reported their find to the authorities. Police dredged the lake and recovered the body, which was identified by the golden barrette.

The dog never returned.

A Call from Uncle Andy

The idea of phone calls from the dead may seem outlandish, but while they don't exactly clutter up the phone lines, they are not as uncommon as one might think. Many people have received calls that seem to come from another world.

Once such phone call was experienced by Ida Lupino, who was a movie star during the middle of the twentieth century. Although Ida became famous in Hollywood, she had been born and brought up in England, a member of a theatrical family that went back for generations. Her father and mother, Stanley and Connie Lupino, were well-known performers in the English variety theater. When Ida was nine, they were living in London at her grandmother's house.

One night, Ida had a disturbing dream about a man she called Uncle Andy, a friend of her parents. She woke up, and went downstairs to tell her grandmother, who was preparing a late supper for Stanley and Connie. While Ida was telling her grandmother about her dream, the phone rang. Her grandmother asked Ida to answer it.

"I went to the phone," Ida relates, "took it off the hook and heard a voice on the line. But it was so faint I could scarcely understand the words. Finally, the voice became stronger and I could understand the message, repeated monotonously several times: 'I must talk to Stanley. It is terribly important.'"

The little girl recognized the voice as that of Uncle Andy. She said her father wasn't home yet. But the voice kept saying the same thing over and over. Ida called her grandmother to the phone. She heard her grandmother say, "Andy, are you ill? I'll ask Stanley to call you the moment he comes in."

Then the call was cut off. Ida's grandmother protested angrily to the operator, who insisted there had not been a call on the line in the past hour.

Stanley and Connie returned a half hour later and Ida told them that Uncle Andy had called. They looked very upset, and tried to send her to bed.

But her grandmother backed her up. "She's not mistaken, Stanley," she said. "I heard Andy too. I think you had better call him. He sounded as though he were ill."

Ida says she has never forgotten how shaken her father's voice sounded when he replied:

"Mom," he said, "Andy is dead. He hanged himself three days ago."

Lord Dufferin's Story

Lord Dufferin, a British diplomat, is the central figure of this story, which has become one of England's classic tales of the supernatural.

One night while staying at a friend's country house in Ireland, Lord Dufferin was unusually restless and unable to sleep. He felt dread that he could not explain, and so, to calm his nerves, he arose and walked across the room to the window.

A full moon illuminated the garden below so that it was almost as bright as morning. Suddenly Lord Dufferin noticed movement in the shadows and a man appeared, carrying a long box on his back. The silent and sinister figure walked slowly across the moonlit yard. As he passed the window from which Lord Dufferin intently watched, he stopped and looked directly into the diplomat's eyes.

Lord Dufferin recoiled, for the face of the man carrying the burden was so ugly that he could not even describe it later. For a moment their eyes met, and then the man moved off into the shadows. The box on his back was clearly seen to be a casket.

The next morning Lord Dufferin asked his host and the other guests about the man in the garden, but no one knew anything about him. They even accused Dufferin of having had a nightmare, but he knew better.

Many years later in Paris, when Lord Dufferin was serving as the English ambassador to France, he was about to walk into an elevator on his way to a meeting. For some unexplainable reason he glanced at the elevator operator. With a violent start he recognized the man he had seen carrying the coffin across the moonlit garden.

Involuntarily, he stepped back from the elevator and stood there as the door closed and the elevator started up without him.

His agitation was so great that he remained motionless for several minutes. Then a terrific crash startled him. The cable had parted and the elevator had fallen three floors to the basement. Several passengers were killed in the tragedy and the operator himself died.

Investigation revealed that the operator had been hired for just that day. No one ever found out who he was or where he came from.

The Navajo Guide

A pioneer family of the Old West settled on the edge of a wide forest. In the woods close by lived a very friendly elderly Navajo couple. The Navajos and the little daughter of the pioneer family were particularly fond of each other.

One winter when the youngster was about six, she started walking through the woods to visit another little girl who lived in a cabin about a mile away. She had gone there alone many times before, so her parents thought nothing of her making the trip again, even though it was winter and it looked like snow. There were few wild animals in the forest, and no wolves had been seen in the area for many years.

A few hours later, when it started getting dark, her parents became concerned. When her father stepped out into the twilight to look for her, he found, to his dismay, that it was snowing heavily. There was no sign of his small daughter.

At once he and his oldest boy bundled up in their heaviest clothes, took a lantern and musket, and started off at a trot down the trail to the other cabin. As they ran along they kept calling the little girl's name, but their only reply was the howling of the wind and an occasional hoot from a great gray owl.

At the neighbor's house they learned that the little girl had left some time ago, before the snow began, and should have arrived home long before. Their alarm mounted. But perhaps, they reasoned, she had left the trail to visit the Navajos' hut.

The girl's brother turned off to visit the couple, while her father and neighbors headed homeward, fanning out through the dark woods to see if they might find the girl before the snow and storm covered up all tracks.

Reaching home first, the men were overjoyed to find the little girl safe by the fire, drinking hot broth while her mother dried her clothes. She had lost her way, she told them. After stumbling in the drifts for a while, she had started to cry. Almost at once her old friend had appeared and led her home, holding her tiny hand in his all the way, until they could see the lights of her cabin ahead. Then he had smiled at her and vanished into the dark woods behind them.

Her brother returned from the Navajos' hut with a sad tale. There, he said, he had found the man's wife huddled by the body of her husband, who had died two days before.

4

Seafaring Frights

The Phantom Captain

He was a tall, broad-shouldered man with an unmistakable air of command, a barrel chest, and a vivid scar that curved across his temple and down his left cheek. On a January night in 1902, the men in the wheel house of the James Gilbert all saw him clearly.

They felt the blast of spray as the tall man forced open the wheelhouse door and spoke to them as they struggled with the buffeting wheel. The three-masted ship was beating through monstrous waves on the 4,600-mile run from the Cape of Good Hope to Bombay.

The order given by this stranger with captain's rings on his sleeve saved the lives of seventy-four men who were within a few hours of a hideous death from starvation and exposure. But at the very moment the crew saw him and heard him speaking, his body was floating lifeless on the storm-tossed waters of the Indian Ocean.

Of this there is no doubt. Nor is there any doubt that the story of the phantom captain is one of the strangest of all inexplicable tales of the sea—still discussed when sailors gather to swap yarns.

The James Gilbert was forty years old when it sailed into marine history. Its square rigs and jaunty profile made for a picture-book ship, and when conditions were right, it could still outrun most of the new-fangled steamships riding the watery routes.

In midwinter 1902, the James Gilbert left London with sixty-eight officers and crew, and fifteen passengers bound for Bombay. Captain Frank Carter was in command.

In a heavy overcoat, he patrolled the decks in the bleak evening air, as the vessel slipped downriver toward the sea.

They dropped anchor at Barking Creek. Longboats came alongside with provisions, including live poultry and a dozen sheep, which were quartered in accommodations near the mainmast.

Dawn saw the James Gilbert out in the English Channel, heading west. With a tailwind, good weather, and calm seas, it made excellent time sailing down the coast of Africa. The ship rounded the Cape of Good Hope and veered northeast on the last lap to Bombay.

Six days later, the barometer fell with alarming speed, and within a few hours, the wind had reached gale force. Waves were crashing over the decks. Cabins were flooded, and passengers huddled in the crew's quarters.

A wall of water smashed into the galley, reducing it to chaos. Sails ripped apart, and ropes chafed until they snapped.

On orders of the captain, bags full of oil were hauled out of the main hatch and punctured so that their contents would smooth the water. But the waves were too violent for the oil to have much effect.

For forty-eight hours Captain Carter never left the wheelhouse.

Two men, and sometimes three, were needed to keep the ship on course. Up in the rigging, the sailors risked their lives to shorten the sail that was tearing loose from its lashings.

On the morning of the second day, the storm eased enough to allow the crew to begin clearing up the wreckage.

Then it blew again, although with less ferocity, and Captain Carter went below-decks for a few hours of sleep, leaving the second mate in charge.

In the wheelhouse during the middle watch was the helmsman, assisted by a seaman and an apprentice. The second mate was on the poop deck, supervising a change of sail.

The helmsman, steering the northeasterly course ordered by Captain Carter, was complaining about the quality of the officers aboard when the apprentice nudged his arm. "Pipe down," said the apprentice. "We've got a visitor."

A tall, stocky man in a captain's uniform pushed past the astonished helmsman into the cramped wheelhouse and peered into the compass.

The binnacle light revealed a long and vivid scar running almost the length of the stranger's face. Without looking up, he commanded, "Steer nor' nor'east."

"I'm not taking any orders except the captain's," replied the helmsman indignantly. "He said nor'east."

But the stranger countered angrily, "I said nor' nor'east. And look lively, for every moment counts." Then he opened the door and disappeared onto the deck.

The helmsman didn't know what to do. Should he take the order? The second mate was still out on the deck. Perhaps the man who looked like a captain was a passenger, and was simply transmitting an order from Captain Carter. Satisfied with this explanation, the helmsman spun the wheel. The ship swung slowly into a fresh course.

Captain Carter woke in the early dawn to excited shouting from the deck. He found his crew hurling out ropes to the occupants of four battered lifeboats tossing in the heavy swell on the port side of the James Gilbert.

The lifeboats were secured, and more than seventy men in an advanced state of exhaustion and shock clambered up the sides of the great sailing ship.

"We're from the brig Firebird, sir," one of the ravaged men explained. "The ship caught fire two days ago. She burned down to the waterline, and then went down. You showed up just in time—we couldn't have lasted another hour."

"Is your captain here?" asked Captain Carter.

"No, sir," the sailor replied. "He was killed as we lowered our boats. The mainmast came down and struck him a fatal blow across the head. He was our only fatality."

The survivors went below for food and medical treatment, and the ship continued on its original course. One hour later, a lookout sighted an odd object bobbing in the water off the starboard bow.

It was the body of a man, a broad-shouldered man with a barrel chest and a vivid scar down the side of his face. And the sleeve of his uniform displayed a captain's rings.

Jinxed Ship

One day in 1869 a workman was inspecting a fishing schooner, the Charles Haskell, for possible damage. He slipped on the steps of the companionway leading to the hold, fell and broke his neck, dying instantly. A single mishap like this usually is chalked up to carelessness or coincidence. But this happened in Newfoundland, Canada, where fishermen who face the dangers of northern waters are likely to take every accident aboard ship as a sign that it is jinxed or cursed.

Certainly, the captain and crew of the Haskell believed this. They deserted the ship immediately.

The owner, unable to find anyone willing to sign on, sold the schooner to a Captain Curtis of Gloucester, Massachusetts. The captain was a no-nonsense man who didn't believe in curses. He had some difficulty finding men to work for him at first, but the pay he offered was good and soon he had a crew. The Charles Haskell was back fishing again on the Grand Banks, a series of shoals off Newfoundland.

Everything went well until 1870, when a hurricane struck the Grand Banks. The hundred or so fishing ships gathered there were tossed about like matchsticks. One huge comber lifted the Charles Haskell and hurled it like a battering ram against the Andrew Johnson, which was smashed to pieces, killing everyone aboard. Though badly crippled, the Haskell managed to limp back to port.

Most fishermen would have considered that part of the Haskell's curse. But since it was the Andrew Johnson that went down, the crew felt it didn't apply to them. Once the ship was repaired, it was back on the Grand Banks again.

For six days the crew of the Charles Haskell fished without incident. But on midnight of the seventh day, the watchmen standing guard spied movement in the waters around the ship. As they watched, twenty-six figures wearing rain slickers began rising out of the sea. One by one, they boarded the schooner. Staring straight ahead through eyeless sockets, they took up stations along the ship's railing. There they went through the motions of fishing.

Frozen with terror, the guards were unable to move until the phantoms put away their imaginary nets and fishing rods and returned back to the sea. Then they rushed to the captain's cabin, gabbling out an account of what they had seen.

Captain Curtis couldn't understand a word they were saying. But he saw stark fear in their eyes and ordered the ship back to port at once. It was well on its way by dawn. In the bright light of day the night's terrors seemed foolish. The captain was on the verge of returning to the Grand Banks when one of the crew shouted, "Look!"

Gaping, captain and crew watched as the twenty-six figures in rain slickers again rose from the sea and boarded the schooner. Once more they took up fishing positions along the rail. Finding his voice at last, the captain ordered full sail for port. But fast as the ship went, it could not shake the phantom fishermen. They stayed aboard until the port finally came into view. Then they climbed over the side of the ship. But this time, instead of sinking into the sea, they started walking across the sparkling waters toward the port, where they disappeared.

Who were they? Demons from the deep? The drowned men of the Andrew Johnson? No one took the time to ask. As soon as they docked, captain and crew fled, never to return.

No others came to take their place. The Charles Haskell was left to rot away in its berth. It never sailed again.

Skeleton Crew

In 1881, the bark *Josepha* was sailing in the middle of the South Atlantic en route to Cape Town when the lookout spotted a small vessel some distance away. He aimed his glass and saw what appeared to be a man slumped on the bow.

After hailing was answered with silence, a launch was rowed toward the unidentified craft. But when the seamen reached the drifting relic, they realized that her four-man crew would never be able to tell them what had happened. They were skeletons.

The figure on the bow was still wearing the tattered remnants of an officer's uniform, but it was impossible to determine his rank. His three men, sprawled nearby, presented an even more macabre display, clad in fragments of clothing that crumbled when touched. It was impossible even to tell the ship's nationality, because her name had been erased by weather and salt water.

After studying her design, it was assumed that the ship had been built in England, but there was no flag or insignia to confirm this opinion. The lost ship's destination also remained unknown because her logbook and ship's papers were missing.

The skeleton crew's position—two thousand miles from the nearest land—was no mystery since winds and currents could have taken them on an aimless journey after the last man died.

What is a mystery to this day is the lonely drifter's fate. How long had the small vessel been manned by a crew of dead seamen? How did they perish? What was the boat's next port? And where was the logbook?

Tale of the Strangled Figurehead

The Portuguese seamen who tell this weird tale swear it is true.

During the days of the wooden ships and iron men of the last century, a Portuguese sea captain, engaged to a dark-eyed beauty of the Virgin Islands, was determined to have her likeness made into a figurehead for his ship. The girl was flattered by the suggestion, until he insisted that she be portrayed wearing her bridal gown. This, she said, would bring bad luck to them both.

The young captain scoffed at her superstition. How could the figurehead bring anything but good luck when she was so lovely and the gown so beautiful? Finally, in tears, the bride-to-be consented and posed for the wood carver in her wedding dress. When the figure was shaped and sanded, she agreed that it was a good likeness, even to the bouquet of flowers she held in her hands.

Amid mixed expressions of congratulations and superstitious anxiety from Virgin Islanders, the figurehead was attached to the vessel's prow under the bowsprit. The young captain sailed off on a short voyage that would bring him back just in time for the wedding a few weeks later, but the wedding was never to take place.

On the return voyage, a dark high-seas storm overtook the vessel. For days it was touch-and-go as to whether or not she and her captain and crew would survive.

When the storm finally blew itself out, the crew scrambled over the rigging to inspect the damage. To their dismay, they found that a rope had wound itself about the neck of the beautiful figurehead on the prow. They quickly untangled it, but hesitated to tell the young captain of their discovery. However, the superstitious rumors of the crew soon came to his ears. Spreading all available sails, he raced home to his bride-to-be.

A sad-faced group of friends greeted the ship. A tragedy had taken place, they said, and urged the Captain to hurry to his fiancée's house. There her tearful parents told him that his bride had died the night of the great storm. The grief-stricken man managed to ask how, but almost before they told him, he knew.

She had dressed herself in her wedding gown to have some minor alterations done by the seamstress. She had hurried up to the attic to fetch a bit of silk lace. On the way down the stairs she had tripped on the long skirt and fallen, catching her long, trailing veil on a peg by the stairs. When the parents had found her, she was already dead—strangled by her own wedding veil.

Blackbeard the Pirate

The pirates of old were legendary, larger-than-life characters who lived at sea on ships that they often stole from innocent people trying to make their way to new lands.

Few pirates were more feared than Edward Teach, otherwise known as Blackbeard the Pirate.

Captain of his own ship, Blackbeard punished his men harshly and didn't hesitate to shoot or throw overboard a disobedient sailor.

His murderous, plundering life caught up with him in 1718, when Lieutenant Robert Maynard of England's Royal Navy surprised Blackbeard at the pirate's favorite cove—Ocracoke Inlet, off the coast of South Carolina.

Maynard and his men laid a trap, and the evil Blackbeard sailed right into it. Within minutes, Maynard and Blackbeard were locked in combat, dueling hand-to-hand in a fierce sword fight. The hulking Blackbeard snapped Maynard's sword in half, leaving him helpless. When the pirate raised his cutlass to finish Maynard off, one of Maynard's loyal men snuck up from behind Blackbeard and cut his throat.

Legend has it that even while blood spurted from his neck, Blackbeard kept fighting. It took an additional five shots and twenty stab wounds to finally lay him to rest. Fearing the ferocious pirate might come back to life, Maynard had Blackbeard's head cut off and hung from the ship's bow.

The sailors said that when Blackbeard's body was dumped into the ocean, the head cried out for it and the body swam around the ship three times before sinking.

Ever since, Blackbeard's ghost has haunted the area of his bloody death. Fishermen have reported an eerie, glowing, headless body floating just below the surface of the ocean. And sometimes, around Ocracoke Inlet, Blackbeard's ghost ventures ashore in search of his head!

So what happened to Blackbeard's severed head? After it hung from the bow of Maynard's ship, the head was taken apart. Blackbeard's skull was then coated with silver and used as a most grotesque punch bowl.

5

Visits from the Dead

The Strangers Who Foretold Death

One summer afternoon in the middle of the 1800s, a group of boys left St. Edmund's College, a well-known school about forty miles north of London, for a boat ride.

The outing, which began as a happy outing, was to end in grim tragedy. One of the boys, Philip Weld, was to die in a whirlpool in the River Lea—and by some mysterious and inexplicable process, his father, more than two hundred miles away, was to learn of the death at that very moment from two strangers he met on the road.

There were fifteen boys in the group, and they left school shortly after lunch. At about 5 p.m., Philip was rowing a skiff containing three others when they decided to change places. A boy named Joseph Barron was to get his turn at the oars.

Philip stood up and edged his way to the bow, while Joseph took his place. Suddenly, an unseen current seized the boat and swung it violently to the left. Philip clung to the side of the boat, lost his balance, and fell into the river.

Cries of alarm turned to shouts of laughter as Philip reappeared—the water was only up to his waist. Joseph moved the boat over, and the other two boys prepared to drag Philip aboard.

As they reached out, there was a swirl of water and a cry. Philip disappeared before their eyes!

The alarm was raised and other boats arrived on the scene. They discovered that Weld had been standing on a thick shelf of clay that had given way under his weight and dragged him down to the river bottom.

The teacher in charge sent the students home and contacted Dr. James Cox, the president of the college. Workmen with grappling hooks were called out, but they failed to locate the body. Although recovery operations went on until dark, nothing was found.

The next day, a lock farther downstream was opened, and the movement of the water dislodged the body from its clay tomb.

Dr. Cox did not return to St. Edmund's but traveled to London, and from there to Southampton, to tell Philip Weld's father of the tragedy personally. With a priest, the Rev. Joseph Siddons, he went to Weld's home and saw the dead boy's father walking near the house.

The two men left their carriage and walked toward James Weld. As they approached, Weld said, "You need not say one word, gentlemen. I know my son is dead."

Then he told a strange story. The previous afternoon he had been walking with his daughter along a lane near his house when he suddenly saw his son Philip. The boy was standing on the opposite side of the road between two men dressed in crimson robes.

The daughter exclaimed, "Look—have you ever seen anyone looking so much like Philip?"

Her father replied, "It must be him—it can be no one else."

They noticed as they hurried toward the group that Philip was laughing and talking to the smaller of his companions. Suddenly, all three vanished!

James Weld, certain that the vision signified some impending disaster, went directly home. When the mail arrived, he scanned it with dread, expecting some bad news of his son. But there were only the usual bills and invitations.

"But when I saw you in a carriage outside my gate, I knew without doubt what you had come to tell me."

Dr. Cox asked Mr. Weld if he had ever seen the men in the crimson robes before. He said that he had not, but the faces were so indelibly impressed on his mind that he would instantly know them again.

Dr. Cox then told Mr. Weld of the circumstances of Philip's death—which took place at the very time the vision had appeared.

At the funeral, the father scrutinized all the people who came to pay their last respects to Philip, but the men in the crimson robes were not among them.

Months passed, and James Weld took his family on vacation in Lancashire.

One Sunday, after attending the evening service at the local church, James Weld called on the local priest, Father Charles Raby.

As he waited in the parlor, Weld glanced at the framed portraits on the wall. One, unnamed, pulled him up with a start. The features, the set of the jaw, the shape of the head—he had seen them all before; he knew them as well as he knew his own face. It was the man who had been at his son's side the day he saw him in the lane.

He asked Father Raby about the portrait. He was told it was of St. Stanislaus, a Jesuit saint—the patron saint of drowning men.

The Ghost Who Came Back for Justice

Sometimes a ghost will stay in our physical world to see that justice is done, that its good name is cleared. Richard Tarwell was such a ghost.

Tarwell, a fourteen-year-old boy, worked in the kitchen of a large country house in England, in the year 1730. The owner, George Harris, also had a house in London. One day Harris received a message from Richard Morris, the butler of his country home. Morris said that the house had been broken into the night before and a large amount of valuable silverware had been stolen.

Harris returned, and got the whole story. Morris said he had been awakened in the night by a noise. He hurried to the butler's pantry, where the silverware was kept, and was confronted by two rough-looking thieves. With them, the butler said, was the young boy Tarwell, who it appeared had let them in.

Butler Morris said that the men had overpowered him and tied him up. Then they and the boy removed all the silver and left for parts unknown. Morris had been found by his fellow servants the next morning, none the worse for wear.

Some months later, George Harris awoke to see a young boy standing by his bed. He realized it was Tarwell. He presumed the boy had been hiding in the house since the robbery.

The boy said nothing, just beckoned. As the lad moved, making no sound at all, Harris realized he was seeing a ghost. He followed the boy out of the house to a large oak tree. The ghost pointed to the ground, and then disappeared.

The next morning, Harris had workmen dig where the ghost had pointed. They found the body of Richard Tarwell.

Police were called, and they interrogated the butler, who confessed. He was part of the robbery plot, having let the thieves in himself. While they were taking the silver, the boy Tarwell had heard a noise and investigated. One of the robbers struck the boy and killed him. To cover the crime, they buried Tarwell and tied up their accomplice, the butler, to hide his participation in the robbery.

Even though he was now a ghost, Tarwell was not going to let the butler get away with his death and the ruin of his reputation.

He was successful. The butler was hanged for the crime.

The Waltz of Death

When the West was still wild, one of the few spots of civilization in New Mexico was Fort Union. This military post was manned by rugged soldiers and many young officers. They were very lonely, for there were few women in these parts.

One day a beautiful young woman, a niece of the commandant, came for an extended visit. Every man on the post fell in love with Miranda. This did not make her unhappy. There was little there to interest her except for men, and flirting was her favorite pastime.

One day a very young lieutenant, just out of West Point, was posted to the fort. He immediately fell madly in love with Miranda. For her, he was a new toy.

Fort Union was established to guard pioneers against the Apache Indians, who themselves were fighting to protect their homes and land. One day the young lieutenant was ordered to lead a small party against the Apaches. That night the young man pledged his undying love to Miranda. She answered in kind, hiding a yawn. As though playing a stage role, she murmured, "I will never marry another man."

"That is well," the young man said, "for whatever happens, I will come back and make my claim."

The scouting party was ambushed by the Apaches. Very few soldiers escaped back to the fort, and the lieutenant was not among them. Miranda showed little sign of sorrow. In fact, secretly she was relieved. Within weeks, she announced that she was leaving to marry a rich man back East.

The people of Fort Union held a going-away party. Everyone came in their best clothes. Miranda danced with one man after another.

Suddenly there was a bang! A door had flown open. A cold wind swept the room. A soldier's wife screamed and dropped to the floor in a faint. For a figure stood at the door. An unearthly cry came from its lips as it staggered forward into the light. It was the young lieutenant. His body was swollen, his uniform stained with blood. His scalp was gone. His eyes burned with a terrible light.

The figure lurched toward Miranda and took the terrified, rigid young woman in its arms. Faster and faster they danced! Miranda grew paler and paler. She slipped to the floor. The ghastly figure stood over her. The lights went out.

When the candles were lit again, the figure was gone. Miranda lay dead.

A few days later, a search party returned to the fort. They brought with them, over the back of a horse, the body of the young lieutenant.

6

Lost Souls

The Spirit of Lindholme

During World War II, the Royal Air Force station at Lindholme, England, was not your average fighter base, and British pilots were not the only airmen who flew deadly missions against vital targets in Germany.

There were aviators from many nations based at Lindholme, but the most maniacal of the bunch were from the Polish air force.

Polish fliers lived only to destroy German planes and cities to retaliate for the deaths and incarceration suffered by their families at the hands of the Nazi troops. The eager airmen would fly until they were ready to drop from fatigue, then take off as soon as they awoke from a few hours of sleep, refueled on hot coffee.

One pilot from this highly driven crew perished in a fiery crash, but still would not quit.

One evening in 1945, a Halifax was returning to Lindholme. The encounter had been successful for the enemy. German anti-aircraft gunners had severely damaged the heavy four-engine bomber.

But the plane was not the only victim of the attack. The pilot was seriously injured, bleeding from several wounds and barely managing to keep the airplane level as it approached the field.

Time became another enemy. As the minutes ticked away, the wounded pilot was getting weaker. He found he was having increasing difficulty concentrating on what he knew would be the one chance to land the bomber.

Then time ran out.

Just as he saw the lights of the airfield, the pilot knew he could no longer maintain altitude. He decided to attempt the landing alone and ordered his crew to bail out. When the last crewman cleared the plane, the desperate pilot lined up with the runway. The plane hit the ground heavily and created a giant watery rooster tail as it began skidding.

Whether it was because the brakes failed or the pilot lost consciousness, the huge bomber came to rest in a soggy bog. Moments later, it had completely disappeared, sunk into the marsh. The operations officer added the aircraft to his long list of casualty statistics, removed the dead pilot's name from the daily schedule, and the war continued.

The Halifax was gone forever, but the valiant aviator refused to be taken off the duty roster.

A few weeks after the tragic crash, the base chaplain was startled by an unusual sight. A pilot, wearing a ragged flight suit and bleeding profusely, suddenly appeared and asked for directions to the mess hall. The chaplain wanted to take the wounded airman to the dispensary, but the ghastly figure utterly vanished before he could speak.

On another occasion, an officer was approached by a bloody flier in a torn flight suit who asked for directions to the mess hall—then disappeared.

The war ended, but the late Polish airman still continued with his unrelenting search for the Lindholme mess hall. The gruesome specter was seen for years, until local authorities decided to claim the bog for its peat deposits.

A digging crew discovered the remains of the Halifax while clearing the marsh. The properties of the bog had preserved the bomber and its lone crewman. The pilot's body sat in the cockpit, dressed in the same ragged flight suit seen by so many at the airfield during the past forty years.

He was buried with full military honors and never seen again.

Dead Man's Inn

On September 30, 1980, a dilapidated inn burned to the ground in Tisakurt, Hungary. Although the fire was intentional, no one cared to find the unknown arsonist. The simmering timbers were all that remained of a haunted building that had been a haven of horror for sixty years.

One unfortunate guest described a spine-chilling sight while staying at the inn. The German tourist was frightened senseless one evening when he opened the dining room door. He saw a large table surrounded by ten rotting corpses, each holding a glass of wine. They were wearing ragged clothes from the Roaring '20s and their lips were curled back, revealing a hideous grin.

Then everyone at the table slowly turned to face him and raised their glasses in a toast to the dead. The terrified man ran away and never looked back.

The citizens of Tisakurt knew what had happened and were

relieved to see the haunted house finally destroyed. Perhaps the evil inn's grisly legend had also perished in the smoldering ashes.

It all began in 1919 when Lazio Kronberg and his wife Susi faced a bleak future after spending all their savings to keep the inn open. Poverty was just another direful circumstance they would have to accept after suffering several other tragedies. Their youngest son and daughter had run away from home years ago, and two older boys had died during the recent war.

There was only one way to escape bankruptcy. The desperate innkeepers decided to pursue a new venture that would satisfy their creditors. Although apprehensive about resorting to crime for survival, they thought it was the only solution, and so, bought bags of quicklime and poison.

Lazio told curious guests the quicklime was going to be used for a new outhouse, while Susi explained that the strychnine would eliminate pesky rats.

Lazio filled a large trench with quicklime, but the offensive rodents never dined on strychnine soup. The poison was added to glasses of wine and served to the Kronbergs' guests during dinner. The victims' valuables were then removed before the bodies were tossed into the trench. Local authorities estimated that ten unfortunate customers enjoyed their last glass of wine at the inn before the summer of 1922.

The last candidate for the quicklime trench signed the inn's register on August 14, 1922.

"Just call me Lucky," said the jovial salesman in his thirties. "I've been very successful and now I'm searching for investment property. In fact, I'm thinking about settling here in Tisakurt."

After dinner, Lazio had an unusual feeling about Lucky and did not want to harm him. But Susi objected furiously. She had been eyeing the new guest's heavy suitcase and was sure it contained money or jewels.

They served Lucky the strychnine sherry and waited impatiently for him to collapse. Susi's suspicions proved true, and

Lazio was thrilled to find the suitcase filled with gold. He also found a faded photograph at the bottom of the bag.

Lazio and Susi studied the photo and soon recognized it as a picture of the Kronberg family that was taken years ago.

The two innkeepers were horrified to discover they had just killed their long-lost son, Nicholas, who ran away when he was nine years old. He had become a prosperous salesman and told his friends he was going back home to surprise his parents with a gift of gold coins. He drank the fatal glass of wine before revealing his true identity.

Lazio and Susi were found in the same position as the grotesque diners who were seen by the German tourist. The murderous couple penned a complete confession before joining Nicholas at the table. They drank a glass of strychnine wine and were found by the villagers three days later.

The inn was operated by several owners before and after World War II. Each proprietor admitted seeing the ghosts of Lazio, Susi, and the murdered guests who ate their last meal at the sinister inn. The ghastly visions were still being seen where so many came to spend the night and never checked out.

Evidence in the Graveyard

Eerie things are sighted in graveyards, but few of them remain in place for all the world to see. A heinous crime, which occurred in Washta, Iowa, in Cherokee County at the turn of the twentieth century, was followed by one of the most ominous sights ever seen on a tombstone!

Heinrich and Olga Schultz, husband and wife, were a kind, elderly couple who lived on a small farm in Iowa. They were well liked and had no enemies. In fact, neighbors and townspeople all respected and admired the Schultzes because of their honest nature and willingness to help other people.

Therefore, it was a sickening shock that they were murdered in cold blood, in the middle of a frigid winter night. Their bodies were found in their home—their heads split open with an ax! There were signs everywhere of a struggle. Heinrich and Olga had fought hard to save their lives, but unfortunately lost the battle. When the townspeople heard the news of their brutal deaths, they shivered with outrage ... and fear.

Three days before his death, Heinrich had withdrawn his life savings from the bank, feeling it would be safer at home. When the bodies were found, the money was gone—along with the Schultzes' hired hand and boarder, Will Florence. Everyone, including the authorities, was convinced that Will had murdered the couple and stolen the money. Will had always been a troublemaker, but Heinrich had felt the need to give him a chance by offering him work around the farm.

An aggressive manhunt ensued, and Will was finally found hiding out in Nebraska. The police couldn't get their hands on enough physical evidence to convict him of the murders, so he was released.

In the weeks to come, a strange phenomenon began to unfold at the graveyard where the Schultzes were buried. A face began to appear in the marble of the joint headstone that the couple shared. Over the course of three or four weeks, the picture grew clearer and clearer. Just as film under chemical action develops a negative, the marble tombstone developed the picture of a face. Rumor of this event circulated, and eventually, law enforcement officials visited the graveyard. Even the most skeptical detectives gasped in shock when they saw it. The perfect likeness of Will was etched into the tombstone.

Several months later, new evidence implicating Will Florence as the murderer surfaced, but although an enormous search took place, he was never found. To this day, however, his guilt remains stamped upon the marble tombstone atop the Schultzes' grave, which still stands in Cherokee County.

Joe Baldwin's Lantern

During the 1800s, the nation's railroads were run by strong, dedicated men who were proud of their profession and heritage. Folk heroes such as Casey Jones and John Henry are known to everyone, but no one remembers Joe Baldwin. He was not an engineer or steel-driving man. Joe was a conductor for the Wilmington, Manchester, and Augusta Railway that operated through Georgia and the Carolinas.

One spring evening in 1868, he was aboard a freight train that was roaring through a raging storm to reach a siding and allow an express to pass.

Joe was sitting in the caboose when he suddenly felt the car slow down. He looked out the window and was astonished to see that the caboose had separated from the train.

The shrill whistle of the approaching express filled Joe Baldwin with terror. He saw its blinding light racing toward him. He grabbed a red lantern, ran to the rear of the platform, and frantically waved a warning signal. He was still standing there when the express slammed into the caboose and exploded, covering the scene with a flaming shroud of wood and twisted steel.

Joe Baldwin's mangled body was found the next morning. His head was missing and never recovered. More than a century later, his headless spirit is still seen walking along the tracks west of Wilmington, waving a red lantern.

Skeptics will tell you the strange glow comes from automobile lights on Highway 87. The strange effect appears under certain atmospheric conditions when headlights are reflected off clouds to resemble a lantern. None of the experts, however, can explain how the eerie image appeared during the nineteenth century, when cars didn't exist. Most railroad veterans are sure the persistent phantom is Joe Baldwin searching for his head.

The Strangling Hands

The phantom hands clamped around the child's face, and the room was filled with the chill of death. William Bayles, standing over his daughter's cot, could see the dents in her flesh made by the force of the invisible fingers.

William Bayles and his family had for weeks been terrorized by a presence they called "It," a malignant being that had transformed their cottage near West Auckland, in England's County Durham, into a house of fear. During the spring of 1953, It first arrived at the cottage, where Mr. Bayles, a forty-year-old garage owner, lived with his wife and young daughter.

First, It lurked outside. "We heard a shuffling out in the garden," Mr. Bayles later told investigators. "This occurred for some nights, and then gradually 'the Thing' seemed to nose its way into the house and become mixed up with our lives."

The Bayleses were not easily frightened, but the presence that infiltrated their home filled them with bewilderment, and finally, with terror. Eventually the presence made itself felt every night.

The family couldn't sleep. Furniture was moved, clothes and books disturbed. One night, Mr. Bayles's wife Lottie was grabbed by unseen hands and pulled across the room. Often when the family retired for the night, they found the beds were warm—as though something had already been lying on them.

The family cat refused to remain in the house at night. Mysterious knocks and clatters disturbed even the most sound sleeper.

The final horror came one night when their young daughter, Doreen, was asleep on her cot in her parents' room. Mr. Bayles later described in detail a scene he would never forget.

"First we felt It arrive in the usual way. Everything became chilled and there was a peculiar odor, the smell of a decaying jungle. Then I noticed that Doreen had begun to struggle in her sleep. As we watched, one of Doreen's eyes was forced open and then the other. It was as if someone was forcing them open with a thumb and forefinger. We could see the marks of the fingers on her skin.

"Lottie and I clung to each other, terrified. Then I forced myself to go over to the cot and pry the hands away. I am sure they meant to murder the child.

"I swept my fist over Doreen's face and at once her head fell back onto the pillow, her eyes closed, and her skin resumed its natural folds."

But there was no sleep for Lottie and William Bayles that night. As the dawn was breaking, they vowed that they had suffered enough. If the Thing wanted them to leave their home, they would.

By now, the haunted cottage had become famous. A group of psychic investigators, intrigued by the reports, asked whether they could spend a few days at the place. The Bayles family agreed. They had already found a new home and wanted nothing more to do with the cottage.

In June 1953, two men, equipped with tape recorders and infrared cameras, installed themselves in the haunted room. They locked the door and waited.

A report compiled the next day reads as follows: "We both fell asleep but were awakened by the sound of something soft plopping about on the floor outside the door. There was a silence and then a pawing sound at the bottom of the door.

"We opened the door and dashed out onto the landing. Our flashlights revealed a curious green haze which drifted eerily near the ceiling. We were conscious of a horrible smell, a smell of decay and rottenness.

"We returned to the room and locked the door. We both had the impression that someone—or something—was on watch outside the door the whole night. With the first light the gaseous smell disappeared and the fumbling sounds went away.

"This convinced us that the watcher on our threshold was a creature of darkness and could not face the clean morning air."

The investigators left the cottage none the wiser, leaving an archaeologist to advance the most reasonable explanations of It.

He suggested that the cottage was built over an ancient well that, under certain conditions, gave out a pungent gas that drifted through the floor of the cottage. As it moved, it disturbed the foundations, creating both the smell and the noises.

But why did they disappear at dawn? How do you explain the episode of the "phantom hands"? How were furniture and belongings physically moved?

These are questions no one can answer. The tale of "It" will remain a classic example of the inexplicable—stranger, indeed, than fiction.

7

Dangerous Demons

A Dangerous Spirit

When Edd Schultz graduated from divinity school, he became a minister in an Episcopal church in Weymouth, a village near Boston. With his wife Caroline and baby Christopher he moved into an old house on the edge of town.

The house had two apartments on the second floor. There was a stairway between them that led down to the front door of the building. Although summer that year was extremely hot, the stairway was always very cold. It was something the Schultzes didn't think much about—at first.

But mysterious, frightening things soon began to happen. One day Caroline was standing at the top of the stairs, holding the baby. Suddenly she felt hands on the back of her shoulders, pushing her. With the baby, she fell twenty steps down the stairs. As she was falling, she could feel a cold chill around her, but she was aware of a warm glow from the baby in her arms. Neither she nor the baby was hurt.

A week later, during the middle of the night, the baby started screaming from his crib in a nearby room. Edd usually got up during the night to attend to the baby, but Caroline could not awaken him. So she got up and went to see what was wrong.

"As she was leaving our bedroom," Edd recalls, "I woke up. I had what I can only describe as a feeling of tremendous panic. I felt I was being held down by an evil presence. It was as though it was trying to possess me."

After a few moments, Edd managed to free himself and follow his wife down the corridor. She had been having her own experiences. She again felt icy hands on her shoulders. They closed around her neck as though trying to choke her. She broke loose and rushed to the baby's room. She picked him up and managed to calm him.

Edd recalls, "It was such a strong experience that to this day we prefer not to talk about it. It sends shivers up and down our spines."

Edd began to question the landlady about the history of the house. He discovered that the house had originally been a barn where a man had committed suicide by hanging himself from a rafter. His body had hung undiscovered for days, in the space that now was the staircase.

Evil on the Cliffs

The chalk cliffs of Beachy Head tower nearly six-hundred feet above the gray water of the English Channel. It is the loftiest headland in southern England, a lonely spot in Sussex in which few people care to loiter—for Beachy Head has a grim history and a macabre reputation.

High among the chalk crags, where the wind always howls even on the balmiest summer day, dwells the most malevolent spirit in Britain. It is an evil influence that, during the past twenty years it is claimed, has hurled more than one hundred victims over the edge to death on the cruel wave-lashed rocks below.

Many have stated positively, some under oath, that they felt this evil influence on the cliffs and had to violently combat a power attempting to force them over the edge to their doom.

Few can stand near the edge of Beachy Head without being aware that some almost hypnotic power lurks in its towering cliffs. A few years ago, a young girl stumbled back hysterically from the Head and up to a patrolling policeman. She said that while she was resting on the cliffs, a cold shadow suddenly descended around her. She felt herself in a strange, dank atmosphere—even though the sun was shining brightly at the time.

She got up and began to run, and "some huge menacing form seemed to follow me, driving me toward the edge of the cliffs." Screaming for help, she turned and ran away from the cliffs—to safety.

The belief that there is an evil influence luring people to hurl themselves over the cliffs of Beachy Head has been common gossip in Sussex for at least four centuries. Local people agree that the cliffs have a strange and menacing atmosphere. "The soft deceptive chalk seems always waiting to hurl you headlong downward," says a local fisherman.

The influence of the mysterious power extends even beyond the cliffs. A nearby manor house has for centuries been visited regularly by disaster and plagues that have from time to time killed off scores of animals, and even taken their toll of human life.

In fact, it is from this house that the trouble is said to stem. When Britain's monasteries were dissolved in 1538, monks from a nearby abbey took refuge in the manor. The story goes that the owner of the manor betrayed their hiding place. The monks were said to have laid a curse on the man, his family, and his possessions. This, say the local people, is the cause of the malevolence that lurks on the cliffs and in the surrounding districts.

For centuries, people in the district had left the phenomenon alone. But in 1952 a group of people gathered on the cliff top intending to exorcise the evil spirit once and for all.

About a hundred people accompanied medium Ray de Vekey to the top of Beachy Head on a wild night in February. By the light of pressure lamps, they gathered to try to contact the spirits of some of the people who had committed suicide there. But then, in a macabre scene unprecedented in occult research, the medium was suddenly attacked by a presence that urged him to jump over the cliff himself.

De Vekey said afterward that the spirit was fully visible to him. It was an elderly bearded man wearing an ankle-length robe like a monk's habit, with black markings on the back.

"It was in chains," said the medium. "Not handcuffs, but ancient wrought-iron shackles. I don't think anyone could have jumped from the cliffs in chains like that. I imagine it was the spirit of someone who had been bound and thrown from the cliffs centuries ago."

The séance began in the ordinary way, with de Vekey calling on the spirit to make some sign he could recognize.

Suddenly he walked toward the edge of the cliff out of the light of the lamps. The watchers moved forward in alarm.

They heard de Vekey shout, "There is a voice calling 'Oh Helen.' There is a George Foster being called." Then, "Peggy Jordan destroyed herself here ..."

"There is a bearded man," de Vekey continued, his voice rising above the wind. "He is evil. He is calling us a lot of blaspheming fools. He is saying he will sweep us all over ..."

The medium began to laugh wildly. Four men rushed forward

to restrain him from hurling himself over the cliff edge. Apparently possessed, he struggled desperately with his rescuers.

"This thing wants revenge," he shouted. "He wants his own back. He has lain in wait for years." His struggles became more violent; then suddenly de Vekey went limp and was dragged back to safety.

After the séance, de Vekey explained: "This was the strongest influence I have ever encountered. I seemed impelled toward the cliff edge. The specter was of someone who was chained, perhaps the victim of a sacrifice, who has hated and wished ill to all ever since."

A week later, the group again climbed the cliff and de Vekey said prayers. This time nothing unusual happened. The medium said, "I think the unquiet spirit has been laid to rest forever."

But has it? Several years later, two climbers claimed they felt a "malign presence" hovering over them as they walked along the downs behind Beachy Head. Is the mysterious evil thing that lurks high above the sea gathering strength to claim more victims?

Gas Brackets

Eileen Nye, who has since moved to Australia, tells this frightening story of an incident that took place during her days in England. When her work took her to a small English village, Eileen was delighted. It was quiet and peaceful, a perfect place in which to bring up her eight-year-old daughter.

Eileen found a delightful old gabled house, rented it at once and moved in with her daughter. She chose a charming little room for the child. Though it now had electric lights, it once had been lighted by gas. The old brass brackets still decorated its walls, adding a quaint old-fashioned touch to the room.

Mother and daughter settled into their new home, adjusting easily to the village life. There was just one flaw. A few days after they moved in, the little girl began complaining of a sore throat.

Then one night Eileen woke up to muffled screams coming from her daughter's room. She rushed in and found the child sitting upright in bed, clutching her throat with one hand and pointing with the other to something in the corner of the room. Eileen couldn't see anything there. When the child tried to explain, only garbled sounds came out.

The next day Eileen took the little girl to the village doctor, who couldn't find anything physically wrong, except for one peculiar fact: there were marks on her throat that looked like thumb prints.

That night, something told Eileen to check on her daughter, though she had heard nothing. When she went into the room, the child seemed to be sleeping peacefully. But there was something strange that made Eileen come to the bedside to get a closer look. The little girl's eyes were wide open. She wasn't sleeping—she was unconscious!

Eileen rushed her daughter to the doctor, who admitted the child to a nearby hospital for treatment and observation. Perhaps, he suggested to Eileen, the key to the child's condition might not lie in a physical ailment but in the past of the old house. Why not check into its history?

Eileen followed his advice. She was horrified to discover that a former tenant, now dead, had strangled his wife in the bedroom Eileen's daughter was using. He had then hung the body from one of the brass brackets, perhaps to make it look like a suicide.

Eileen moved out of the house at once and her daughter recovered completely. But the village doctor believes she had a narrow escape in the old house. It's his opinion that if she had stayed in that room another night, she would surely have died at the ghostly hands of a dead strangler.

Killer Tree of the Cameroons

All that was left of the campfire was a smoldering glow deep in the wood ash, but Bob Fellows, huddled snugly in his sleeping bag beneath the old tree, didn't notice that, in the last few moments before the African dawn.

Something had roused him from his sleep, and for a moment he lay there wondering what was wrong. Then he heard a rustling noise from the tree above his head, and a few moments later, a weird, gurgling moan. Thinking that there might be a leopard or some other animal about to attack, he snatched up his flashlight and rifle and turned to waken his partner, Mike Cura.

That was when he saw it. Mike Cura's sleeping bag had been ripped to shreds and there wasn't a sign of him. Then something whipped through the darkness and smashed against Fellows' shoulder.

The blow sent him spinning across the ground and half stunned him, but a choked scream brought him to his senses. The cry came from up among the branches of the tree, and training his flashlight on them, Fellows saw a horrifying sight.

His partner's body was being slowly and powerfully crushed to death by the branches of the tree. One branch had wrapped itself around his throat and was strangling him, while several other, thicker ones were exerting such pressure on his body that Fellows could almost hear the bones splintering.

Then, slowly, when the life had been squeezed out of the victim, the grotesque killer tree unraveled its branches and let Cura's body fall limply to the ground.

Fellows remained where he was, too horrified and too frightened to move, as the uncannily armlike branches groped blindly toward him. But they couldn't quite reach him.

Fellows stood there until the first streaks of daylight. The tree gave a heavy, shuddering sigh, and its branches seemed to lose their life.

Four days later, in May 1903, Fellows was telling police in Iloku, in the Cameroons, that his partner had been murdered

by a tree! Of course, the authorities didn't believe his story.
Fellows was held on suspicion of murder, while an expedition
set out to recover Cura's body.

When the body was brought back to Iloku, an inquest was
held, but the results of it were so startling that they were not

made public for many years. Fellows was, however, freed from
jail and the charge was quietly dismissed. For the doctors who
carried out the postmortem stated that Fellows could not have
killed his friend; the damage had been inflicted by some pow-
erful, super-human creature. One doctor said that he doubted
if even a gorilla would have possessed the strength to mutilate
a body so severely.

Shortly afterward, a missionary working in that district
heard about Cura's death and wrote Iloku authorities about
similar incidents.

Apparently, twelve men had been found dead at the base of
that tree within a period of fifty years, and for centuries the
African tribesmen had treated that particular stretch of forest
as taboo.

The origins of the legend were based on a tribal priest
about eighty years earlier, a man named Ubo, who suddenly

went berserk and started a campaign of terror in the region. Many people were waylaid by him and strangled to death for no reason at all.

At last the warriors set out to hunt the killer down. They trapped Ubo beneath the tree one evening during a thunderstorm. As they closed in for the kill, there was a flash of lightning. The tree was struck, and so was Ubo, who had been standing with his back to the trunk. When the tribesmen recovered his body, they found that both his hands had been sliced off at the wrists by the lightning. Yet the warriors couldn't find the missing hands anywhere.

It was soon after that, according to the missionary, that the tree started to gain the reputation of being a "strangler" tree.

But that wasn't the end of the story.

Less than six months after the death of Mike Cura, a boy from the mission school staggered into Iloku to gasp out an incredible story to the police. The missionary had been killed by the tree—right before the boy's own eyes.

The boy had gone with the missionary to chop down the tree and destroy it once and for all. But they hadn't arrived there until late evening, and while the boy started a camp, the missionary approached the tree with an ax.

Even before the blade hit into the tree trunk, the boy heard the missionary scream in terror. He turned just in time to see thick branches wrapping themselves around the man's body.

The police inspector who went to investigate found the dead missionary hanging limply in a fork in the tree trunk. By then it was morning and the tree seemed nothing more than just a dead tree.

However, the inspector and his patrol had instructions to destroy it—which they did. With a loud groan, the mighty trunk crashed to the ground. Then it was chopped and sawed into logs that were piled in a heap to be burned.

Before this could happen, a strange and gruesome discovery was made. As one of the soldiers split a log, he found two human, skeleton hands trapped within the wood. Both hands had been severed at the wrists.

8

Without a Trace

The One They Couldn't Bury

No one seems to know much about the origin of this tale, except that it happened "way out West" and "way back when." The setting was in a rough-and-ready cattle-raising area where law and its enforcement were often swift and abrupt, though not always accurate. Hangings by lynch mobs were common. They were the almost inevitable punishment for cattle and horse thieves, crop burners, and mine-claim jumpers.

For several months before this incident took place, cattle had been disappearing from the local herds. Suspicion finally fell upon an old codger who lived alone up a canyon a few miles outside of town. He didn't have any cattle, nor could people figure out what he had done with them, but they suspected him all the same. The case against him was simply that no one else was available to blame.

Small groups of men gathered in the saloons and talked about what could be done to stop the thefts. Some of them insisted that they couldn't take justice into their own hands without some proof that the old man had taken the cattle. At least, they might try catching him in the act. Others held that they had to hang somebody for the crime.

As the cattle continued to vanish, feelings grew hotter, until one day the mob got completely out of hand and headed for the little hut where the old man lived. They found it empty, but as they were leaving, up strolled the old chap, leading his horse. A fresh cowhide was tied to his saddle. There, apparently, was evidence enough that he had been killing cows and skinning them for their hides. This would explain why people had never been able to find any live cattle about his canyon or any other signs that he had been stealing them.

The old codger stoutly maintained his innocence. He said that he had found a single dead cow and had skinned it because it did not have a brand on it. The mob examined the hide and, sure enough, could find no brand. But a section of the cow was missing—that part where a brand might easily have been located. This was proof enough for the mob, and they hurried the old man down the mountain to the small town.

In order to make this a spectacle for the instruction of other possible cattle thieves, they decided to erect a scaffolding and hang him in style, instead of just throwing a rope over a convenient tree. The old chap maintained that even if they did hang him they'd never bury him as a cattle thief, and swore long and loud to that effect while they hammered the scaffold together in the town square.

When all was ready and the crowd was waiting, the gang leader sprang the trap. The old man had spoken the truth. He fell through the trap opening but never was actually hanged. The empty noose swung crazily in the air—for the victim had vanished. A cold gust of air whipped over the crowd about the scaffold. Neither the old man nor the missing cattle were ever seen again.

Did Michael Norton
Fall Through a Hole in Time?

One of the most uncanny stories I have ever come across concerns the baffling disappearance of a Canadian farmer's son, twelve-year-old Michael Norton, on a November morning over sixty years ago. The hunt for the missing child went on for years, because although he disappeared physically, both his parents and hundreds of investigators all heard Michael's voice—calling faintly from the same few square feet of ground.

On the day it happened, Michael overslept. When he rushed down to breakfast, he was seen by his father and mother, an aunt, and two farm workers. A few minutes later his mother watched him trudge toward the cow shed. She had no way of knowing that neither she nor anybody else would ever see the boy again.

Some hours later, wondering about his absence, Ruth Norton called Michael to come back to the house or he would be late for school. Michael's younger brother and sister were impatiently waiting for him to take them into the village.

There was no answer to Mrs. Norton's call and, with some irritation, her husband put on his boots and went out to fetch the boy. When he entered the barn, it was empty. The stool and bucket were there, the latter half full of milk. Michael had obviously stopped in the middle of his work—but there was no sign of him.

Mr. Norton searched the barn. He found nothing. He called his family and the workmen and they combed the farm and its environs. There was no trace of the boy.

Seriously alarmed, Mr. Norton drove into the nearby township of Burtons Falls and alerted the police. A few hours later, the police arrived at the farm with a bloodhound, which was given Michael's scent. The animal's keen nose soon detected Michael's trail. It led from the kitchen door into the barn and then out of the barn again, straight into the open south pasture, a field visible from both the house and the nearby road.

Then the bloodhound, which had been tugging excitedly at

the leash, suddenly stopped in its tracks. They were in the middle of the pasture, several dozen yards from the farther boundary. Surprised, the handler urged the dog on, but the animal just whined. The trail had disappeared!

What happened? No one ever found out. Search parties were organized and other tracker dogs brought, but none of them ever uncovered a hint of the boy's movements after he had stood in the middle of the field. Michael Norton had literally disappeared into thin air!

A few nights later, when hope of finding their son alive was fading, the Nortons were overjoyed to hear a voice outside. It was Michael's, and it called one word that no other boy would call in that place: "Mom!"

They rushed outside, shouting with relief, and then stopped. There was no one there! The voice called again, "Mom!" It was Michael, both were certain of that. But they searched and searched and found nothing. They called his name and he didn't answer. Half an hour later, as they stood in the farmyard, peering hopelessly into the dark, they heard him again: "Mom," and this time he clearly added, "where are you?"

Many people came to the little farm, and many of them heard the lost voice as it called and pleaded for help. One of the most logical theories that was put forth suggested that he had tumbled into an underground river, an old well, or simply a crack in the ground. But this idea was eventually discarded when experts studied the terrain. A primitive form of aerial photography was also used, hoping to pinpoint a fault in the field. But there was no evidence to suggest such a thing.

For weeks, the frantic parents and others heard the disembodied voice of Michael Norton, which was growing fainter as the days passed. It seemed that he was in a thick mist, but quite free to move. Then, after a while, he was heard no more.

Is it possible that some unknown physical law opened a "gap" in time, through which Michael fell or was pulled? And that such a suspension of the normal laws would be visible to the human eye, maybe as a "mist," or some other alteration of the light?

Might it be this disturbance that Michael saw? Might he have run across the field to see for himself, and been swallowed up in the middle of the pasture, which was, for a brief moment, the "eye" in the needle of time?

9

Stranger Than Fiction

The Creepiest Confession

In the early 1800s, an unsuspecting Mexican priest heard a dreadful confession . . . from a dead man. The encounter, which occurred in Mexico City, proved to be the most tormenting experience of the priest's life and went down in history as one of the creepiest confessions ever told.

One stormy winter evening, Padre Lecuona hurried through the stinging rain to the house of a friend. On his way he heard the voice of an old woman call out to him: "Padre, please wait. You must hear a confession. It is urgent, we haven't a moment to lose!" The priest, eager to arrive at his destination, answered, "Surely one of the other priests can attend to this matter."

"Oh no," declared the woman. "He asks for you—and only you!"

The woman led the padre to a dilapidated, darkened house in an alley. As he followed her through the door, a wave of foul air assaulted him. The woman lit a candle. In the flickering glow, he could see the form of an emaciated man lying flat on his back on the floor in the corner.

As the priest knelt down, he sensed something was wrong. The man's skin was brown and leathery, stretched tightly over bones. The head was but a skull scarcely covered with skin and a few wisps of matted hair.

"Mother of God!" gasped Padre Lecuona. "This is no living man!"

Suddenly, the figure rose to a sitting position and croaked, "Forgive me, Father, for I have sinned." In a raspy voice, the corpse recounted how, years before, a gang of thieves had broken into his home, stolen all of his possessions, and murdered him and his wife with a hunting knife. Because he died so quickly, he was never able to receive his last rites by a priest.

Now, the man claimed, through divine intervention, he had been permitted to return and make his confession.

Horrified at what he was seeing and hearing, the priest

quickly forgave the man for the sins in his previous life. When he was finished, the man crumpled into a mummified corpse. The priest fled the house at once and began looking for the old woman in hopes of getting an explanation for the bizarre occurrence, but she had disappeared.

The next day, still in shock, Padre Lecuona and a friend returned to the house in the alley. The door looked as if it had not been opened in years. Cobwebs stretched over it, even over the rusted keyhole.

Could the entire incident have been a dream? Distraught, the men broke into the house. Inside they saw only a vacant room. "Hello?" the men called, but their voices echoed through the empty house.

As Padre Lecuona turned to leave, he saw a handkerchief lying in the corner where the corpse had been. It was the one he had been carrying the night before. As he bent to pick it up, a sharp pain shot through his chest, and a wave of dizziness engulfed him.

"Are you all right?" the priest's friend asked in alarm.

"I think so," answered the padre, but those were the last words he ever spoke. The priest clawed at the door, opened it, and then stumbled out into the alley.

Three days later, after lapsing into a state of delirium, the padre died. Doctors were never able to find a cause or reason for his tragic demise, but when the house was demolished years later, a moldy, crumpled, mummified skeleton (the corpse who confessed?) was found behind one of the walls.

The house where the supernatural confession took place sat in an alley in Mexico City. Soon after the padre died, the townspeople dedicated the alley to the priest by naming it Callejón del Padre Lecuona (meaning the Alley of Father Lecuona), which it is still called today. It is said to be a dark and dangerous place, haunted by evil spirits.

The Pilot Who Saw a Dread Future

Throughout history there has been evidence that at times some people have caught glimpses of the future. Often these pictures of approaching events come in dreams. But they are also seen by people who are fully awake. Take the experience of George Potter, a Royal Air Force pilot during World War II.

Wing Commander Potter was stationed at a base called RAF Shallufa in Egypt. From this base, bombing planes flew out over the Mediterranean Sea to plant torpedoes and mines in the paths of ships carrying supplies to the North African desert forces of the German General Erwin Rommel. This was a crucial period of the war, the first time the Allied armies were winning. They were pushing back the forces of the Germans' most successful general, known as the Desert Fox.

The airmen's missions were extremely dangerous. Between bombing runs there was much nervous gaiety as they tried to forget the peril of their lives. They ate, drank, sang, and laughed as though they were schoolboys, which they had been not long before.

One evening, Commander Potter entered the Officers' Mess with a friend, Flying Officer Reg Lamb. At a nearby table, a group of flyers were celebrating something—perhaps that they were still alive. One of them was a wing commander whom Potter refers to as Roy.

After a few moments, Potter heard a loud burst of laughter from the table, and glanced over that way. As he has described it:

"I turned and saw the head and shoulders of Roy moving ever so slowly in a background of blue-blackness. His lips were drawn back from his teeth in a dreadful grin. He had no eyes in his eye sockets. The flesh of his face was blotched in greenish, purplish shadows."

A few seconds later, Potter felt Reg Lamb tugging at his sleeve. "What's the matter?" Lamb asked. "You've gone white as a sheet. You look as if you've seen a ghost!"

"I have seen a ghost," Potter replied. "Roy over there has the mark of death on him."

Lamb looked over at the table of joking officers, but could see nothing unusual.

That night Roy was shot down. He and his crew were seen clambering into a life raft, but the air-sea rescue planes were unable to find them. The flyers were never heard from again.

"I then knew what I had seen," Potter relates. "The blue-black background was the sea at night, and Roy was floating in it, dead, with his head and shoulders held up by his life jacket."

Voices of the Dead

On a warm summer evening in 1949, the four children of Captain and Mrs. Roland Macey finished their high tea in the paneled dining room of Fresden Priory, a rambling mansion that had once been a monastery.

The children ran through the open French windows and out onto a small flagged terrace where their mother was sitting with the local priest.

"Mother," said the oldest child Mary, who was twelve years old, "can we go upstairs and listen to the singing?"

"What is that?" the priest inquired.

"Oh," said the mother, "they say they can hear singing up in the nursery, but of course it is all nonsense."

It turned out, however, that what the Macey children could hear was anything but nonsense. It was what psychic researchers call a "mass echo in time," and certainly the most uncanny and well-documented example of "voices from the dead" ever reported.

For years, authorities on the paranormal had sought proof for the centuries-old belief that antique furniture or wooden altars used for mass had the power to transmit through time the Latin chanting of monks who lived hundreds of years before. Now, it seemed, the four Macey children were going to provide that proof.

The priest asked permission to accompany the children up to the nursery. There he saw a large table standing against a wall. The children stood beside the table and immediately became completely absorbed.

Although the priest could hear nothing, he asked them to try singing along with what the children called the "funny music," and they did.

When he returned downstairs, the priest told Mrs. Macey, "What your children can hear, but we cannot, is the sound of the monks who lived here five hundred years ago, singing their evening office. It is archaic plain-chant Latin, completely unused today."

The children knew no Latin, were not Roman Catholic, and had never even heard a Latin mass. So when they repeated what they had heard "the table singing," there was no way to doubt them.

But children, it seemed, were the only ones privileged to hear the chanting monks.

A team of experts arrived with high-frequency recording equipment and heard nothing. The table itself was examined and carefully taken apart, revealing a false top. Underneath was a wooden frame with a stone cross set in it.

It was an altar used for secret masses when Catholicism was illegal in England.

Dr. William Byrne, a medical student with a fine reputation as a psychic investigator, heard about the singing at Fresden priory. He asked for and was granted permission to visit the house. Once again, the children repeated the words they heard coming from the table. Some teenage cousins visiting the house also claimed that they could hear the singing.

Late one evening, after making a series of unsuccessful tests in the house, Dr. Byrne and two assistants were walking across the drive to their car when they became the first—and last—adults to hear the voices of the dead.

"We heard," Dr. Byrne was to explain later, "the sweet singing of ghostly monks. It was so clear on the air that at first I thought it was a radio turned on. But it was not. Then I realized we were below the window of the room in which the altar stood.

"For over half an hour, the chanting continued. Almost afraid to move, I reached out to switch on a portable tape recorder I was carrying.

"Suddenly the singing stopped. Then I heard the voice of a man slowly reading. The voice came from the thin air about twenty feet from me and was in some archaic form of Latin."

Then there was silence. Dr. Byrne clicked off his recorder and wound back the tape. The spools revolved—and only a quiet hiss emerged from the speaker.

The voices were, it seems, beyond the range of any man-made equipment.

How can the past be transmitted to us through inanimate objects?

Roger Pater, a well-known expert on the occult, explains it like this: "Anything that has played a part in events that aroused very intense emotional activity seems to itself become saturated, as it were, with the emotions involved—so much so, that it can influence people of exceptional sympathetic powers and enable them to see or hear the original events almost as though they had been there."

Is this the explanation for the phantom voices of Fresden Priory? It probably is—at least until someone can think of something better!

INDEX